TUCKAHOE SCHOOL
LIBRARY
6550 No. 26th
ARLINGTON, VA 22213

P9-CFQ-054

APPLE

Nikki McClure

Abrams Appleseed, New York

FALL

FIND

SNEAK

HIDE

SECRET

HELLO

SHARE

FORGET

QUIET

RETURN

WAIT

PREPARE

PLANT

SPRING

THE LIFE OF AN APPLE TREE

Apple seeds rarely grow into trees that make tasty apples. But every so often they do. It takes about ten years for an apple tree to get big enough to grow apples. Once the tree is ready, it waits all winter with cold, bare branches. Then the tree bursts into bloom in the spring. Bees visit the pink-tipped flowers and carry pollen from tree to tree. The base of each flower swells to form an apple, and the petals fall off one by one. All summer, the tree grows and the apples get big and round. In the fall, the apples begin to drop from the tree. They are ripe and ready for picking and eating. Then the wind blows the leaves away, and the apple tree is left with bare branches once more to wait for the spring.

COMPOSTING

After the little girl leaves it on the playground, the apple in this book ends up on the compost heap. Compost is food for plants. You make compost by collecting scraps from the table and garden into a pile or bin. Apple cores, coffee grounds, grass clippings, leaves—food and plant bits like these go into the pile, along with layers of soil. All winter, worms, insects, and tiny bacteria break down the scraps into little nutritious pieces. They create the compost. Compost is rich with the food that plants need to grow. In the spring, compost can be added to a garden to help the plants grow bigger. Sometimes seeds in the compost end up sprouting in the garden, too, just as one does in this book.

WINTER

SPRING

SUMMER

FALL

FOR STELLA AND CYPRESS

This book was originally made in 1996. While on a walk, I discovered an apple tree loaded with fruit. That night, I took black paper and drew a picture of an apple falling from a tree. I then cut out the image using an X-Acto knife. It was my very first paper cut, and it is the first picture in this book. When I had enough pictures for a little book, I printed and bound copies by hand and sold them through local bookstores. Now *Apple*, my first book, is enjoying a second life in this edition.

Cataloging-in-Publication Data has been applied for and may be obtained from the Library of Congress.

ISBN 978-1-4197-0378-2

Text and illustrations copyright © 2012 Nikki McClure

Book design by Chad W. Beckerman

Published in 2012 by Abrams Appleseed, an imprint of ABRAMS. All rights reserved. No portion of this book may be reproduced, stored in a retrieval system, or transmitted in any form or by any means, mechanical, electronic, photocopying, recording, or otherwise, without written permission from the publisher. Abrams Appleseed is a trademark of Harry N. Abrams, Inc.

Printed and bound in U.S.A.
10 9 8 7 6 5 4 3 2

For bulk discount inquiries, contact specialsales@abramsbooks.com.

ABRAMS
THE ART OF BOOKS SINCE 1949
115 West 18th Street
New York, NY 10011
www.abramsbooks.com

TUCKAHOE SCHOOL
LIBRARY
6550 No. 26th
ARLINGTON, VA 22213